For my honey-bunny

Distributed in Canada by D&M Publishers, Inc.

Color separations by Chroma Graphics PTE Ltd.

Printed and bound in November 2010 in China

by Macmillan Production Asia Ltd., Kwun Tong, Kowloon, Hong Kong

(supplier code 10)

Designed by Jaclyn Sinquett and Natalie Zanecchia

First edition, 2010

1   3   5   7   9   10   8   6   4   2

www.fsgkidsbooks.com

Library of Congress Cataloging-in-Publication Data

Jahn-Clough, Lisa.

Felicity & Cordelia : a tale of two bunnies / Lisa Jahn-Clough.— 1st ed.

    p.   cm.

Summary: Felicity Rose and Cordelia Bean are best friends, but they are separated when Felicity wants to go on a hot air balloon trip and Cordelia does not want to accompany her.

ISBN: 978-0-374-32300-4

[1. Best friends—Fiction.   2. Friendship—Fiction.   3. Hot air balloons—Fiction.   4. Voyages and travels—Fiction.]   I. Title.

PZ7.J153536Fe 2010

[E]—dc22

2009016143

Felicity & Cordelia: A Tale of Two Bunnies

Lisa Jahn-Clough

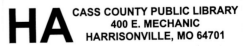
FRANCES FOSTER BOOKS · FARRAR STRAUS GIROUX · NEW YORK

"Let's go for a ride in the hot air balloon,"
said Felicity. "I want an adventure."

"I'll get cold," said Cordelia.

"We'll bring a blanket," said Felicity.

"I'll get hungry," said Cordelia.

"We'll bring some pie," said Felicity.

"No, thanks," said Cordelia. "I prefer pie on the ground."

"I will go by myself," Felicity said.

"What if the balloon breaks?" Cordelia asked.

"I will fix it," Felicity said.

"How will I know you're okay?" Cordelia asked.

"I will write every day," Felicity said.

"What if you drift far away and can't get home?" Cordelia asked.

"I will find a way," said Felicity.

Felicity packed paints, paper, envelopes,
stamps, and a large piece of pie.
"Off I go!" she called.
The balloon began to rise.
"Goodbye, Cordelia! Goodbye!"

"Goodbye, Felicity! Goodbye!"
Cordelia watched the balloon until it was
just a tiny dot in the sky.

"I hope she doesn't drift far away," Cordelia said.
"I hope she comes home soon."

At suppertime Cordelia watched the sky.
There was no sign of Felicity.
Cordelia set the table for two, just in case.
"I hope she has enough to eat. I hope she
is warm," Cordelia said.

Cordelia went to bed and dreamed of Felicity.

As the balloon went up, up, up, Felicity watched her
house until it was just a tiny dot on the ground.

The clouds rolled by. The sun began to set.
"It's too bad Cordelia isn't here to see this," said Felicity.
She took out her paper and began to paint.

Soon it got dark and the wind picked up.
"I wish I had an extra blanket," Felicity said.

"And another piece of pie," she added.
She fell asleep and dreamed of Cordelia.

Felicity woke with a bump.
She had landed far away.

"Oh, no," she said. "I must write to
Cordelia so that she doesn't worry."

Back home, Cordelia woke with a bump.
She looked around for Felicity, and then
remembered she wasn't there.

"Maybe Felicity will come home today," Cordelia said.
Cordelia tidied up so that everything was perfect.

At the same time, Felicity traveled high and
low in search of a mailbox.

Finally, she found one.

At lunchtime a letter arrived for Cordelia.

Dear Cordelia,
Here is a picture
of me at sunset.
The balloon broke,
but I am fine.
Love, Felicity

P.S. The pie was yummy!!!

Cordelia
Bunny Grove,
12345

"It looks like Felicity is having quite an adventure,"
said Cordelia. "But she should have taken more pie."
On the back of the letter was Felicity's painting.
Cordelia set about making a pretty frame
so she could hang the painting on the wall.

The next day another letter arrived.

Dear Cordelia,
Here I am in the
hills! It is cold.
I will find a
way home soon!
Love, Felicity

P.S. I wish I had more pie!

Cordelia
Bunny Grove,
12345

"Oh, dear," said Cordelia. "She should have
taken an extra blanket."
Cordelia spent all afternoon picking berries
and making pie.
She watched the sky every so often.
"It is time for Felicity to come home," she said.

But Felicity could not fix the balloon.
She was tired and hungry.
Suddenly she got a whiff of something yummy.
"It is time to go home," she said.

Cordelia was taking pie out of the oven
when a package arrived.

It was so big that she could barely lift it.

Cordelia cut the ribbon.

"Surprise!" said Felicity.

"Yay! You're back!" said Cordelia. "I was worried."

"There's always a way home," Felicity said.

"And there's always pie," Cordelia said.

"Perfect!" they both said.

That evening, Felicity and Cordelia watched the sky.

"I'm glad you're home," said Cordelia.

"Me, too," said Felicity.

They went inside for more pie.
"Let's go scuba diving," Felicity said.